# SUPER CHICKEN NUGGET BOY

## vs. Dr. Ned-Grant and His Eggplant Army

by JOSH LEWIS
illustrated by DOUGLAS HOLGATE

𝔇isnep • HYPERION BOOKS
NEW YORK

For Sarah & Mira—
My Number One Nuggets

Text copyright © 2010 by Josh Lewis
Illustrations copyright © 2010 by Douglas Holgate

First U.S. edition
1 3 5 7 9 10 8 6 4 2
V567-9638-5-10258

This book is set in 13 point Excelsior.

Printed in the United States of America
Library of Congress Cataloging-in-Publication Data on file
ISBN 978-1-4231-1529-8 (hardcover)
ISBN 978-1-4231-1534-2 (paperback)
Reinforced binding

Visit www.hyperionbooksforchildren.com

# 1

## EGGED ON

Dr. Myron Ned-Grant, Approved Certified Food Scientist, was one of the most successful people ever to attend Bert Lahr Elementary School.

He was the first person to discover that chocolate and ground beef don't taste good together, and he was the inventor of the thirty-pronged fork, which allowed people to eat an entire twelve-course meal in one bite. He was also the guy who came up with the sound *Gllll,* after he determined that people were getting tired of always only saying, *"Mmmmm,"* after they ate something tasty.

It was twelve twenty-two. All the students of Bert Lahr Elementary School were sitting in the auditorium, writing down questions to ask Dr. Ned-Grant. Dr. Ned-Grant was at the school to talk to the students for their monthly *Graduates of Bert Lahr Elementary School Who Have Jobs That We've Never Heard of Before* series.

Allan Chen's question was . . .

"WHY IS SQUASH CALLED SQUASH WHEN IT'S NOT EVEN SQUASHED?"

Donna Wergnort's question was . . .

Second grader Finneus Washington's question was . . .

Finneus hadn't been paying attention when his teacher, Mr. Hirdleman, told the class that a *food* scientist was coming to speak to them. Finneus thought Mr. Hirdleman had said a *nude* scientist, as in, no clothes.

Fernando Goldberg, better known as Fern, thought long and hard about what to ask Dr. Ned-Grant. He wanted to ask him what a giant chicken nugget could do to avoid extreme flaking during long, hard-fought battles, but he realized that that might give his secret identity as Super Chicken Nugget Boy away, since everyone had to write their names on their paper. So instead he wrote . . .

On the other side of the room, Dirk Hamstone laughed his evil little laugh, "Heh-heh-heh," as he wrote down his question.

WHICH CAME FIRST, THE DOUGHNUT OR THE BAGEL?

Dirk's sidekick, Snort, snorted along with Dirk: *Snort! Snort! Snort!*

Snort had no idea what they were laughing about, but he didn't care.

Dirk turned to Snort, annoyed. "What's so funny?" he asked.

"I don't know," said Snort. "What's so funny to you?"

Dirk smiled a wicked smile. "You'll see."

Principal Hamstone stood up on the stage and introduced Dr. Ned-Grant. "Dr. Myron Ned-Grant is not only Gordonville's greatest living food scientist, he's also a graduate of

5

Bert Lahr Elementary School and, I'm proud to say, one of my first students."

The students clapped while Dr. Ned-Grant stood up and took a bow. Principal Hamstone mixed up all the sheets of paper with questions on them and stacked them into a big pile so that everyone in the school had an equal chance of getting their question answered.

Principal Hamstone pulled a sheet of paper from the pile. "Our first question for Dr. Ned-Grant comes from Kurt Lenses in the third grade," he said, reading the name off the top of the page. "Kurt asks, 'What was your first invention, and how did you do it?'"

Dr. Ned-Grant smiled and said, "My first invention I created when I wasn't much older than you are now, and I did it using everyday ordinary food coloring. That invention, Kurt, was none other than the Rainbow Salami."

The students all gasped, "Aaahh."

Principal Hamstone pulled another question off the pile. "Terrific. Our next question is from fifth grader Sissie Majors. Sissie asks, 'What are you working on now?'"

"Well, Sissie," said Dr. Ned-Grant, "I'm working on a number of different projects at the moment. I'm working on an all-string-cheese diet that I call the All-String-Cheese Diet. I'm also working on a way to eat breakfast before you wake up. And finally, I'm building a truck made entirely out of jelly."

"Ooh," said the students. They were very impressed.

"All righty, moving right along," said Principal Hamstone, grabbing another sheet of paper. "Our next question is from Fernando Goldberg in the fourth grade."

Fern's friend Lester McGregor nudged him.

Fern smiled and thought about how he was happy that he hadn't written down his first question, the one about Super Chicken Nugget Boy. That would've been weird.

Principal Hamstone began to read from the paper. "'Did you become a food scientist because . . .'"

Wait a second! Fern thought. That's not my question.

Principal Hamstone continued, "'. . . Because your last name rhymes with *eggplant*? Ned-Grant, eggplant, get it?'"

The students burst into laughter.

Dr. Ned-Grant's face turned bright red.

Principal Hamstone shook his head in disappointment.

Fern wondered how his name had gotten on that question.

On the other side of the room, Dirk giggled

with delight. "*That's* what's so funny," he said to Snort.

"But how did you know he was going to write that question?" asked Snort.

"Because *he* didn't write it," said Dirk. "*I* did."

"Ohhh . . ." said Snort as he realized what was going on. *Snort! Snort! Snort!*

The students continued to laugh as Dr. Ned-Grant turned redder and redder.

He finally opened his mouth.

Dr. Ned-Grant's voice echoed through the school, down the street, and throughout Gordonville: "N-O-O-O-O-O-O-O."

The kids looked at Dr. Ned-Grant in shock. The power and fury of his voice was like nothing they'd ever heard before.

Principal Hamstone turned to Dr. Ned-Grant. "You okay, Myron?" he asked in a low voice.

"Yes, Murkwood," Dr. Ned-Grant answered quietly. "I'm just . . . um . . . well . . . yes . . . I'm fine."

But, as anyone could see, Dr. Ned-Grant was far from fine.

# 2

## STICKS AND STONES MAY BREAK MY BONES, BUT DON'T EVER CALL ME AN *EGGPLANT*

s he drove home after his visit to Bert Lahr Elementary School, Dr. Ned-Grant pounded on the steering wheel and screamed at the top of his lungs.

See, the truth is, Dr. Ned-Grant actually *did* become a food scientist because his last name rhymed with eggplant. But it's a little more complicated than that.

When Dr. Ned-Grant was a boy, kids at Bert Lahr Elementary School used to tease him about his name.

It got so bad even Dr. Ned-Grant's teachers started accidentally calling him Eggplant.

Dr. Ned-Grant spent years trying to get over the pain and humiliation he had suffered at school. The first thing he had to deal with was all the rage he felt toward the world, and especially toward eggplants.

Next, Dr. Ned-Grant had to deal with all the sadness he felt about what he had gone through.

Finally, it came time for Dr. Ned-Grant to get on with his life.

Dirk Hamstone knew all about Dr. Ned-Grant's eggplant issues, because his father, Principal Hamstone, had told him.

# 3

## D. TENSION

Fern sat in the front row of the detention room.

Principal Hamstone had given Fern two days of detention for the Dr. Ned-Grant incident, even though Fern had told him that he wasn't the one who'd written the question.

Not far from Fern, Mr. Pummel sat behind his desk.

"WHAT WAS THAT?" Mr. Pummel barked out. "WHAT DID YOU JUST SAY?"

Fern looked around to see who Mr. Pummel was yelling at. But Fern was the only other person in the room, so he figured Mr. Pummel was yelling at him.

"Um . . . nothing," said Fern.

"You sure about that?" asked Mr. Pummel.

"Yes," said Fern. Fern was absolutely sure he hadn't said anything.

Dirk and Snort entered the room. They were there because Dirk's dad, Principal Hamstone, had given them a year and a half of detention for creating a Furious Fry to attack the school with.

"Well, well, well, look what we've got here," said Dirk.

"Yeah. *Snort! Snort!*" said Snort. "Look what we've got—"

"PIPE DOWN, YOU TWO!" Mr. Pummel hollered at Dirk and Snort. "You know the rules: PLANT IT! SIT UP! And SHUT DOWN!"

Dirk and Snort dropped their heads, walked to the back of the room, and sat down.

But before too long, Mr. Pummel was asleep, with his head buried in his newspaper.

This isn't so bad, Fern thought. I don't see what the big deal is about detention. You just sit here.

Then Dirk started in. "Psst . . . worm," he whispered. "Psst . . . psst . . ."

Fern ignored him.

Dirk whispered, "I never thought I'd see the day when Mr. Goody Two-shoes himself would end up in detention."

"Yeah," whispered Snort. "Goody Two-shoes himself! *Snort!*"

"What are you doing in here, anyway?" whispered Dirk.

Fern didn't answer. He knew better than that.

"I asked you a question," whispered Dirk. "Answer me."

Fern stayed silent.

"What's the matter?" Dirk whispered. "Stupid Chicken Nugget Boy couldn't get you out of detention? Heh-heh-heh . . ."

*"Snort! Snort!"*

They were starting to get to Fern, but he did his best not to show it.

"Oh, wait, now I remember why you're here," said Dirk. "It's because you wrote that dumb question about Dr. Ned-Grant."

Hearing that made Fern furious, since he

*hadn't* written that question about Dr. Ned-Grant.

"I mean, calling him an eggplant!" said Dirk. "Even I'm not that stupid."

"An eggplant!" said Snort. "Incredible!"

That did it! Fern couldn't take it anymore! "I didn't call him an eggplant!" he shouted.

Mr. Pummel suddenly bolted out of his chair, got right up in Fern's face, and started screaming his head off. "WHAT DO YOU THINK YOU'RE DOING? DO YOU ACTUALLY THINK I CAN'T HEAR YOU! DO YOU? DO YOU? DO YOU? HUH?"

"But he . . ." said Fern, pointing at Dirk.

"*BUT HE! BUT HE! BUT HE!*" said Mr. Pummel. "GIVE ME A BREAK! DO YOU LIKE DETENTION? IS THAT IT? BECAUSE IF YOU DO, I CAN GIVE YOU PLENTY MORE, YOU GOT THAT, MISTER? YOU GOT THAT?"

Fern could hear Dirk and Snort cackling quietly in the back row.

"Ha-ha-ha."

*"Snort, snort."*

"WHAT ARE YOU SNORTIN' ABOUT? PUT A SOCK IN IT!"

"But—" Snort protested.

"BUT NOTHING!" said Mr. Pummel.

Dirk continued to laugh.

"YOU, TOO!" Mr. Pummel screamed at Dirk.

"But my dad is—"

"I DON'T CARE IF YOUR DAD IS THE QUEEN OF ENGLAND! YOU'RE UNDER MY RULE NOW!"

Fern sighed. He was beginning to understand what the big deal was about detention.

# 4

## THE FRUIT FACTOR

By the time Dr. Ned-Grant went to bed that night, he had completely forgotten about the earlier eggplant incident.

But he wouldn't forget for long.

A spooky voice called from the darkness of Dr. Ned-Grant's room. "Myyyyyrrrrronnnn . . . Myyyyyrrrrronnnn."

"What?" answered Dr. Ned-Grant, lying in bed half asleep.

"Myyyyyrrrrron, wake up," the voice called.

"Leave me alone," said Dr. Ned-Grant, not even bothering to open his eyes.

"Open your eyes now, Myron Eggplant!"

"What did you just call me?"

"You heard me, Eggplant!"

Dr. Ned-Grant shot up in his bed. "Who are you?" he called out. "Show yourself!"

"Turn on a light and I will!"

"Okay," said Dr. Ned-Grant, "you're on!"

He flipped on his night light.

"Wuh!" he gasped as he found himself face to face with an oversize eggplant sitting upright on the chair in the corner of his room.

"What do you want from me?" Dr. Ned-Grant asked the eggplant.

"It's not what I want *from* you. It's what I want *for* you," said the eggplant. "For us."

"And what might that be?"

"Revenge," said the eggplant. "Revenge!"

"But I don't want revenge."

"That's just the problem. If it were up to you, you'd let those Bert Lahr bozos call you Eggplant for the rest of your life. You'd let the entire world call you Eggplant!"

"That's not true," said Dr. Ned-Grant.

"Is too," said the eggplant.

"Is not!"

"Is too!"

"Is not!"

"Is too!"

"This is ridiculous! I can't believe I'm sitting here arguing with an eggplant," said Dr. Ned-Grant.

"Don't change the subject!" said the eggplant.

"Fine," said Dr. Ned-Grant. "So what do you want me to do about it?"

"You must first seize control of Bert Lahr

Elementary School and then . . . Conquer the world!"

"What?!"

"It's the only way people will finally learn to honor and respect eggplants in the way that we deserve to be honored and respected."

"You're crazy! I won't do it!" said Dr. Ned-Grant. "Absolutely not."

"Do you really want those Bert Lahr brats making fun of you for the rest of your life?" asked the eggplant.

"I don't care," said Dr. Ned-Grant.

The eggplant started softly chanting, "<sub>Myron Eggplant . . . Myron Eggplant . . .</sub>"

"That's not going to work," said Dr. Ned-Grant.

The eggplant got louder. "Myron Eggplant . . . Myron Eggplant . . ."

"You're wasting your time. That doesn't bother me."

The eggplant started shouting. "MYRON EGGPLANT! MYRON EGGPLANT!"

Dr. Ned-Grant's lips started to quiver.

"MYRON EGGPLANT!"

Dr. Ned-Grant's body started to shake.

"MYRON EGGPLANT!"

Dr. Ned-Grant covered his ears.

"MYRON EGGPLANT!"

Dr. Ned-Grant started breathing heavily.

"MYRON EGGPLANT! MYRON EGGPLANT!"

"No!" Dr. Ned-Grant yelled out. He started to drool. "Enough! Please! Stop!"

But the eggplant didn't stop.

"MYRON EGGPLANT! MYRON EGGPLANT!"

Dr. Ned-Grant pressed his hands against the sides of his head in agony. His hair stood up straight.

"MYRON EGGPLANT! MYRON EGGPLANT!"

A demonic expression came over Dr.

Ned-Grant's face as he screamed, "AAAAAAAAAAAGHHHHHHHH!!! I'LL DO IT! I'LL DO IT! I'LL DO IT!"

The eggplant stopped chanting.

Dr. Ned-Grant stood there panting and twitching and growling, his hair standing on end. The eggplant had driven him insane. He was now a full-fledged mad food scientist.

"I knew you'd come around," said the eggplant. "I just knew you'd come around."

# 5

## ROUGH SMOOTHIE

Fern sat in the front row of the detention room, staring out the window at Lester and Roy Clapmist. They were on the playground playing one of Fern's favorite games: Who-Can-Spin-Around-in-Circles-Until-They-Fall-Over-or-Throw-Up-or-Both?

*Thump.*

Fern felt something hit the back of his neck.

He turned around.

Behind him, Dirk was sitting reading a book, *How to Make Enemies and Annoy People*, while Snort slept at his desk.

Fern turned back to face the front of the room.

*Thump.*

Another something hit Fern, this time on his shoulder.

Fern turned around again. Dirk was still reading, and Snort was still sleeping. This time, though, Snort seemed to be snorting in his sleep.

Fern resumed facing front.

*Thump.*

He felt something hit him in the head. He turned around.

"Stop!" he whispered to Dirk.

"What?" Dirk said.

"Yeah, we weren't throwing pieces of erasers at you," Snort said, suddenly miraculously waking up.

"HEY! HEY! HEY!" yelled Mr. Pummel.

"WHAT'S GOING ON OVER THERE?"

"They're throwing things at me!" Fern said to Mr. Pummel.

"IS THAT TRUE?" Mr. Pummel asked Dirk and Snort.

"No!" said Dirk.

"No!" said Snort.

"ALL RIGHT, WELL, THERE YOU GO," said Mr. Pummel. "TWO AGAINST ONE. NOW PLANT IT! SIT UP! AND SHUT DOWN!"

"That's not fair," said Fern.

"YOU WANT FAIR, GOLDBERG? HOW ABOUT A WHOLE MONTH OF DETEN-TION? HOW'S THAT FOR FAIR? WHAT DO YOU THINK OF THAT IDEA, HUH?"

"I don't want a whole month," said Fern. "I just want—"

"THAT DOES IT!" said Mr. Pummel,

heading over to his detention book. "YOU JUST BOUGHT YOURSELF—"

Suddenly a loud noise echoed through the school . . .

Followed by a scream . . .

"Aaahh!"

And then robotic laughter . . .

"HA-HA-HA!"

"WHAT'S THAT RACKET?" asked Mr. Pummel. And then it came again.

*Splash!*

"Aaahh!"

"HA-HA-HA!"

"What the heck . . ." Dirk said.

*Splash!*

"Aaahh!"

"HA-HA-HA!"

"It's coming from over there!" said Fern, pointing to the window.

Everyone ran to see what was going on.

"Smoothie Assault!" yelled Snort.

Dirk, Snort, Mr. Pummel, and Fern looked out the window at one of the most frightening sights they'd ever seen—a great big Blenderbot running rampant around the playground. If you've never seen a Blenderbot before, you're lucky. If you have seen a Blenderbot before, then you know that a Blenderbot is an enormous combination blender-robot, capable of unleashing treacherous blended concoctions at tremendous speeds with mind-boggling range and thickness.

This particular Blenderbot was spraying students and teachers with gallons and gallons of stomach-churning smoothies.

All around the playground, students were being covered in gobs and gobs of the sickening stuff.

The Blenderbot grabbed a tomato, some macaroni and cheese, a bunch of spinach, and a bologna sandwich from its side-storage-section slot.

It tossed all that food up into its stainless-steel blender head, liquefied it, then removed the lid from its blender head and, with the blade still spinning, unleashed its supersonic smoothie.

Lester and Roy ran to avoid getting soaked by the shocking shake. But it was no use. The power and fury of the Blenderbot's flying food was too great. There was no escaping it.

*Splash!*

"AAAHH!"

they screamed in horror.

"HA-HA-HA!" laughed the Blenderbot in a robotic voice as it drenched everyone with the gruesomely gross mixture. "People and teachers of Bert Lahr Elementary School, I am not here to hurt you. I am just here to conquer you. Surrender now, and be spared the wrath of my sinister smoothie assaults."

This isn't good, Fern said to himself. "May I go to the bathroom?" he asked Mr. Pummel.

"WHAT, AT A TIME LIKE THIS? ARE YOU COMPLETELY OUT OF YOUR GOURD?" said Mr. Pummel. "THIS IS NO TIME FOR POTTY APPOINTMENTS! NOW, GET IT TOGETHER!"

*Splash!*

Outside, four third graders got hit with a beet, beef, and brown-sugar burrito bomb.

"What do we do?" Dirk yelled.

"ALL RIGHT, NOBODY PANIC!" said Mr. Pummel. "I GOT THIS UNDER CONTROL!"

"I really have to go to the bathroom," said Fern.

"THAT'S ENOUGH ABOUT THE BATH-ROOM, GOLDBERG!" yelled Mr. Pummel.

"Yeah!" said Dirk.

"Yeah!" said Snort.

Fern shook his head in frustration.

Mr. Pummel cranked open the window and stuck his head out. "LISTEN HERE, YOU FEEBLE FOOD FLINGER! I ORDER YOU, IN THE NAME OF BERT LAHR AND THE WHOLE GORDONVILLE COUNTY PUBLIC SCHOOL SYSTEM, TO EVACUATE THE PREMISES IMMEDIATELY!"

"AAAHH!" Mr. Pummel screamed as he got smacked right in the face with a pickle, egg, and blueberry blast.

"HA-HA-HA!" laughed the Blenderbot.

Mr. Pummel collapsed to the ground. Dirk and Snort knelt over him.

"Mr. McGillicutty, is that you?" said Mr. Pummel in a little-boy voice. "I'm sorry I didn't deliver your paper yesterday. My dog Burpy got stung by a horsefly." Mr. Pummel had totally lost it. He had no idea where he was or what was going on.

"Looks like now might be a good time for me to go to the bathroom," said Fern, backing out of the room.

"Well, what I'd really like to do, Mr. McGillicutty," said Mr. Pummel in his spaced-out state, "is to learn ballet."

Fern rounded the corner and rushed

through the halls as fast as he could. He knew exactly what he had to do. He just prayed he wasn't too late.

Fern arrived at Ms. Durbindin's room and made a beeline for Arnie Simpson the Salamander's tank.

"Hey, there, buddy," said Fern, grabbing Arnie and pulling him out from under a pile of bark chips. "We've got some work to do."

Fern headed over to Lester's desk. Lester always had extra ketchup packets lying around. Fern grabbed a packet and squeezed it on himself and Arnie.

*Kerplam!*

Just like that, in an instant, Fernando Goldberg and his favorite salamander associate were transformed into Super Chicken Nugget Boy and Arnie the Awesome Amphibian!

"Come on!" said Super Chicken Nugget Boy. "Time to blow away a Blenderbot!"

# 6
## THE SUPER CHICKEN BLENDER BATTLE

By the time Super Chicken Nugget Boy came riding out onto the playground, everyone had been battered and bruised by a blizzard of smoothie bombs.

"Hold it right there, you pitiful, pea-brained appliance!" said Super Chicken Nugget Boy to the Blenderbot. "Just what do you think you're doing?"

"What does it look like I am doing, you pathetic piece of poultry?" said the Blenderbot. "I am conquering this school!"

"Not if I have anything to say about it!" said Super Chicken Nugget Boy. "Giddyup, Arnie!"

Arnie ran toward the Blenderbot, carrying Super Chicken Nugget Boy on his back.

"Then I am glad you do not have anything to say about it," said the Blenderbot as he

flung a kumquat, a waffle, and a cheesesteak
sandwich into his blender head.

The blending sound cut through the air.

*REEEEEEEERRRR!*

"I hope you are hungry," the Blenderbot said, "because it is time to EEAAATTTTT!"

*Wizzzzz* . . .

The smoothie smacked Super Chicken Nugget Boy right off Arnie's back and . . .

*Thud!*

. . . Onto the playground pavement.

"Didn't your mommy ever teach you not to throw food?" asked Super Chicken Nugget Boy.

"I am a robot. I do not have a mommy."

"No wonder you have no manners," said Super Chicken Nugget Boy. He flung a broken-off piece of his breading at the Blenderbot.

The breading hit the Blenderbot right in the lid, knocking off the top of its blender head and sending the contents soaring.

"Goodness!" exclaimed the Blenderbot. "That is some mighty crispy breading."

"Have you had enough?" asked Super Chicken Nugget Boy. "Or are you hungry for more?"

"I have had enough," said the Blenderbot.

"Good," said Super Chicken Nugget Boy. "Now put your lid on and get out of—"

*Wizzzz . . .*

Before Super Chicken Nugget Boy could finish his sentence, the Blenderbot reached into its side-storage-section slot, chucked some chow into its blender head, and slammed Super Chicken Nugget Boy with another shot of extremely severe smoothie.

*Splat!*

Super Chicken Nugget Boy went flying and smashed into a tetherball pole.

*Bonk!*

He fell.

"Hey," said Super Chicken Nugget Boy, "you said you had had enough."

"I have had enough. But that doesn't mean that *you* have. HA-HA-HA!"

*Splat!*

The Blenderbot hit Super Chicken Nugget Boy with another blast.

*Splat!*

And another.

*Splat!*

And another.

*Splat! Splat! Splat! Splat!*

"HA-HA-HA!" the Blenderbot laughed.

Super Chicken Nugget Boy lay on the ground, exhausted and overwhelmed from the thrashing he was getting. Bits and pieces of his breading were scattered around the playground, including a giant chunk of his belly breading, which rested about ten yards away from him. He wanted to pick up the breading and heave it at the Blenderbot, but he was just too beaten down.

"Do you give up yet?" asked the Blenderbot.

"I never leave the table until I've finished

everything that's in front of me," said Super Chicken Nugget Boy. "Is that all you've got?"

"No. There is plenty more where that came from. This is an all-you-can-eat smoothie spray."

The Blenderbot unleashed its biggest, most colossal blast yet.

*Wwwiiiiiiiiizzzzzzzzzzzzzz . . .*

As the smoothie sailed upward, Super Chicken Nugget Boy cried out, "Arnie! The belly! The belly, Arnie!"

Arnie the Awesome Amphibian sprinted over to Super Chicken Nugget Boy's broken-off belly breading, snatched it up with his salamander teeth, then flicked it from his mouth and into the hands of Super Chicken Nugget Boy.

Super Chicken Nugget Boy positioned the broken-off belly breading in front of him like a shield and prayed that he had just the right angle to make his scheme a success.

The smoothie splashed onto the breaded nugget belly.

*Doyngg!*

The smoothie ricocheted off the crispy

breaded barricade and flew back at the
Blenderbot.

"Oh, dear!" The Blenderbot tried to escape,
but there was no way it was going to dodge
the smoothie.

*Splat!*

"OUCH!"

*Splat! Splat! Splat!*

"OUCH!"

The Blenderbot continued to sprint, and the smoothie continued to splatter, until the Blenderbot ran completely off school property and all the way back to wherever its Blenderbot home was.

Arnie hurried to Super Chicken Nugget Boy's side.

"Good boy, Arnie! Good boy!" said the Super Nugget.

With a deep sigh he looked down at himself and at all the kids and teachers on the playground who were covered in smoothie, and wondered, "Does anyone have any wet wipes?"

# 7

## THE MASTER PLANTS

That night, the psycho talking eggplant appeared once again in Dr. Ned-Grant's bedroom. It was NOT happy about what had happened on the playground.

"You moron!" the eggplant screamed at Dr. Ned-Grant. "How could you let an overgrown fried freak beat your great big bruiser of a Blenderbot?"

"I'd like to see you battle Super Chicken Nugget Boy," said Dr. Ned-Grant. "He's tough."

"I can't battle Super Chicken Nugget Boy," yelled the eggplant. "I'm an eggplant!"

"Excuses, excuses," said Dr. Ned-Grant.

"You're hopeless," said the eggplant.

"Yeah, well, at least I tried. I built a Blenderbot," screamed Dr. Ned-Grant. "You haven't done a thing."

"How can I? I just told you—I'm an eggplant!"

"So? You can talk, and you can appear out of nowhere in people's bedrooms. I don't see why you couldn't also defeat Super Chicken Nugget Boy and seize control of the school and then conquer the world if you wanted to."

"This is ridiculous!" said the eggplant. "I can't believe I'm even sitting here having this conversation. Eggplants can't defeat Super

Chicken Nugget Boy and seize control of the school and then conquer the world! We're too little and too squishy!"

"Sure," said Dr. Ned-Grant. "That's what all the talking eggplants say."

"I don't even know any other talking eggplants," said the eggplant. "And besides, talking isn't important for defeating Super Chicken Nugget Boy and seizing control of the school and then conquering the world! It would be much more helpful if I was a walking eggplant than a talking eggplant. Then I could do battle. But I'm not a walking eggplant, I'm a talking eggplant, so for now you'll just have to—"

"Wait a second," said Dr. Ned-Grant. "That's it!"

"What?"

"That's it! That's it!"

"What's it?" asked the eggplant.

"An eggplant army!" said Dr. Ned-Grant.

"An eggplant army?"

"Yes," said Dr. Ned-Grant. "An eggplant army. What better way to teach the world to respect eggplants than to conquer them with an eggplant army?"

"Sounds perfect," the eggplant agreed. "There's just one problem: where are we going to get an eggplant army?"

"Don't worry," said Dr. Ned-Grant. "I'll think of something. I'm a mad food scientist, remember?"

# 8
## THE DURBINDIN DILEMMA

Ms. Durbindin was the coolest teacher at Bert Lahr Elementary School.

HI. I'M SHIRLEY DURBINDIN. SOMETIMES IT SOUNDS LIKE THEY'RE SAYING MR. BINDIN, WHICH IS FINE WITH ME, BECAUSE I KNOW THAT IT JUST SOUNDS LIKE THAT AND THEY DON'T THINK I'M A MAN.

Ms. Durbindin played games with her class every single day. She played games like Who Can Make the Ugliest Face? and the Pencil Teepee Play-offs, and sometimes she even took her students to the school basement to play Spot a Rat!

Whenever it was somebody's birthday, Ms. Durbindin would bring in her famous Chocolate-Chocolate-Chocolate-Chip-Fudge-Chocolate-Chocolate Cupcakes.

One time, when she was teaching the class about Greek mythology, Ms. Durbindin got everyone, including herself, to dress up in togas and reenact the Trojan War.

For all of those reasons and many more, Ms. Durbindin's students loved her very, very much. Which is why they were all so troubled when one day she suddenly started turning into an eggplant.

It happened right after she returned from the office, where she had gone to make copies of a handout on the history of wigs. She came back into the classroom looking kind of weird and spacey. But that was just the beginning.

Allan Chen immediately noticed the purple color spreading over Ms. Durbindin's usually rosy cheeks. He didn't say anything to Ms. Durbindin about it, though, in case she might have been turning purple as part of some lesson she was trying to teach the class that he hadn't been paying attention to.

That didn't occur to Janice Oglie. She was the second person to notice Ms. Durbindin turning purple. Janice just pointed at Ms. Durbindin and screamed, "Purple!"

Ms. Durbindin looked over at Janice as the purple spread across her forehead.

"Purple!" Janice screamed again.

Ms. Durbindin tried to respond. But it was

no use. She opened her mouth, but nothing came out.

By that point, everyone in the class was staring in shock as Ms. Durbindin's eyelids and ears turned purple.

"Ms. Durbindin!" shouted Roy Clapmist. "Y—y—you're . . . pur . . . pur . . . pur . . ."

"What do we do?" screamed Farnsworth Yorb.

As great a teacher as Ms. Durbindin was, there was one thing she had never taught her students, and that was WHAT TO DO WHEN YOUR TEACHER STARTS TURNING INTO AN EGGPLANT!

It was Fern who finally took control of the situation. He'd been playing with Arnie Simpson the Salamander when he noticed Ms. Durbindin changing colors. He put Arnie down on his desk, walked over to his teacher, and calmly said, "Ms. Durbindin . . . don't be alarmed . . . but you're . . . turning . . . purple."

Ms. Durbindin stared blankly at him, unable to speak.

"Does anyone have a mirror?" Fern asked his classmates as Ms. Durbindin's body started turning oblong.

Everyone frantically searched the room, but there was no mirror in sight.

A green stem popped out of the top of Ms. Durbindin's head.

Winnie Kinney, Donna Wergnort, and Roy Clapmist started to cry.

Just then, Fern noticed something out of the corner of his eye. "Lester! Quick! Hand me that!" he said, pointing to the Roller Coaster

Renegades lunch box under Lester's desk.

Lester threw his lunch box across the room.

Fern caught it and held the shiny clear part up to Ms. Durbindin's face. She caught one glimpse of her eggplant self and fainted.

By the time Ms. Durbindin woke up, she was completely purple, green-stemmed, eggplant-shaped, and still unable to speak. The transformation was complete. She was no longer Ms. Durbindin the teacher. She was Ms. Durbindin the eggplant.

Then, as if things weren't weird enough, Arnie Simpson the Salamander scurried over and started feverishly nibbling away at her eggplant body.

"No, Arnie! No!" yelled Fern as he pulled Arnie off Ms. Durbindin the eggplant.

CHOMP!

CHOMP!

CHOMP!

And now, please welcome back Harvey Zwerkle.

The song is called "Oh, Your Teacher," and it's sung to the tune of "Oh, Susanna."

Remember: This is a sing-along. You have to sing!

Okay, ready? And a-one, a-two, a-one two three!

WHEN YOUR TEACHER TURNS ALL PURPLE
AND SHE GROWS A STEM THAT'S GREEN
AND SHE GETS ALL ROUND AND FAT,
THERE'S ONLY ONE THING IT CAN MEAN.

SHE IS NOT A NORMAL PERSON.
SHE HAS GOT A RARE DISEASE,
WHICH IS WHY SHE SMELLS
LIKE SHE'D BE GOOD
ON TOAST WITH MELTED CHEESE.

OH, YOUR TEACHER
NO LONGER NEEDS HER PANTS,
FOR SHE'S TURNED INTO A JUICY
PURPLE EXTRA-LARGE EGGPLANT!

One more time! ♪

♫ *OH, YOUR TEACHER*
*NO LONGER NEEDS HER PANTS*
*FOR SHE TURNED INTO A JUICY*
*PURPLE EXTRA-LARGE EGGPLANT!*

♩

The students stood over Ms. Durbindin, stunned.

"It just doesn't make sense," said Fern. "I've never heard of anyone turning into an eggplant, ever."

"Me, neither," said Lester.

Allan Chen nodded. "As far as I know, this is the first reported case in history of a human being turning into an eggplant."

That was true. It was. But it was far from the last.

# 9
## AN EGGPEDEMIC

The next day, the first grade teacher, Mrs. Sneap, was telling her class about how her cat, Mr. Pumblechook, loved to watch scary movies on TV.

"It's so adorable," said Mrs. Sneap. "Mr. Pumblechook gets right up close to the TV, and just as something scary is about to happen, he closes his little kitty mouth and holds his breath, like this. . . ."

Mrs. Sneap started holding her breath. The students laughed.

Mrs. Sneap continued to hold her breath.

The students laughed harder.

Mrs. Sneap held her breath even longer.

The students laughed more and more.

The students laughed so hard that nobody noticed that Kenny Brack had returned from the boys' bathroom and promptly turned into an eggplant in the back row.

Over the next few days, dozens more teachers and students turned into eggplants.

Here are some examples of life during the Bert Lahr Eggplant epidemic:

# 10
## ABSOLUTELY NOTHING TO WORRY ABOUT

Principal Hamstone, being the smart principal that he was, could tell that the students and teachers who hadn't been turned into eggplants were starting to worry. So he called an assembly. But when it came time to speak, he could only get out a few words. Then he just stood there looking all weird and spacey.

So Mr. Hirdelman, a second grade teacher, stepped up to the podium to help Principal Hamstone out.

"Principal Hamstone realizes that some of you may be concerned that because your friends and teachers have been turned into eggplants, you might also be turned into an eggplant," said Mr. Hirdelman. "But he's here to tell you that nothing could be further from the truth."

Principal Hamstone's eyelids turned purple.

"Just because your friends are eggplants doesn't mean you will become one, too."

Principal Hamstone's ears turned purple.

"Look at us. I'm a second grade teacher, and he's the principal of the school, and we're not eggplants."

Principal Hamstone's neck and arms turned purple.

"So, stop worrying."

Principal Hamstone's body turned into an oval.

Mr. Hirdelman smiled.

All of Principal Hamstone's outward features were smoothed away and disappeared into the eggplant that he now was.

The students sat and stared at him.

"That didn't make me feel any better," said Roy Clapmist.

# 11
## EGGSPLORATION

Fern and Lester approached the Gordonville International Foundation for Food Findings Building.

"Are you sure you want to talk to this guy?" said Lester. "I mean, I don't think he likes you very much."

"This isn't about me. Something terrible is going on at our school, and he just might be the only one who can help," said Fern.

He knocked on the door.

The door opened, and there stood Dr. Ned-Grant. The moment he saw Fern and

Lester, a huge smile came over his face. "Why, hello," he said.

"Um, sorry to disturb you," said Fern. "We're from Bert Lahr Elementary School."

"Yes, of course," said Dr. Ned-Grant, still smiling. "I remember you."

"You do?" asked Fern.

"Of course. You're the boy who asked that funny question about my name."

"So, you're not mad?" asked Lester.

"Of course not. Why would I be mad? I know it was all in fun."

"Phew, that's a relief," said Fern. "Even though I wasn't the one who actually wrote the question."

"Whether you did or you didn't, it never bothered me in the least," said Dr. Ned-Grant. "What kind of person would I be if I let a silly little joke like that bother me? Now, I suppose you boys are here about the eggplant epidemic."

"Yes," said Lester. "How did you know?"

"Because it's all I've been thinking about since it began," said Dr. Ned-Grant. "It's terrible, isn't it? Nobody wants to see their loved ones turned into eggplants."

Dr. Ned-Grant got very close to Lester and Fern and whispered:

I HAVE A PLAN, BUT WE'D BETTER NOT DISCUSS IT HERE, BECAUSE, WELL, IT COULD BE DANGEROUS.

"DANGEROUS?" Lester repeated loudly.

"Yes, dangerous," whispered Dr. Ned-Grant. "You never know who might be listening."

"Where can we discuss this safely?" whispered Fern.

"Hmm . . . good question," said Dr. Ned-Grant. "How about if we meet at your school, in Arnie Simpson's supply closet."

"Arnie Simpson has a supply closet?" asked Lester.

"Arnie Simpson the janitor, not Arnie Simpson the Salamander," said Fern.

"Oh, yeah," said Lester.

"Shall we say tomorrow at twelve thirty?" asked Dr. Ned-Grant.

"You got it!" said Fern.

"But that's our lunchtime," said Lester.

Fern smacked Lester in the chest.

"Don't worry," Fern said to Dr. Ned-Grant

as he and Lester headed down the hallway. "We'll be there."

"Yes, you will," Dr. Ned-Grant said to himself in a low, evil voice, as Fern and Lester got farther away. "And I'll be waiting . . . waiting to turn you into eggplants! HA-HA-HA!"

Fern heard Dr. Ned-Grant muttering and turned around. "Did you say something?"

"Oh . . ." said Dr. Ned-Grant, caught off guard. "Yes, I just . . . um . . . told myself a funny joke and was laughing at it."

"Oh, okay," said Fern. He and Lester continued walking away.

And that joke's on you, Dr. Ned-Grant said to himself. HA-HA-HA!

# 12
## PLANTS' TRAP

Fern and Lester stood inside Arnie Simpson's supply closet, peeking out through a crack in the door, looking for Dr. Ned-Grant.

Suddenly they found four eyes peeking back at them.

"What are you doing in there?" asked one voice.

"Yeah, what are you doing in there?" asked another voice.

Fern and Lester recognized the voices immediately. They belonged to Janice Oglie and Winnie Kinney. Normally, Donna

Wergnort would have been with them too, but she was now an eggplant.

The last thing Fern and Lester needed was for Janice and Winnie to know that they were meeting Dr. Ned-Grant to discuss his top secret plan to save the school from the eggplant epidemic.

"Don't worry, I'll take care of this," Fern said to Lester as he stepped out of the closet, leaving Lester inside.

"Hi," said Fern.

"What are you doing in there?" asked Janice.

"Yeah, what are you doing in there?" repeated Winnie.

"Uh . . . well," said Fern, trying to come up with a good excuse, "haven't you heard? It's National Spend Some Time in a Janitor's Closet Month."

"I never heard that," said Janice.

"Yeah, I never heard that," repeated Winnie.

"Well, it is," said Fern. "So you'd better find a janitor's closet right away. Too bad this one's already taken. Okay, see ya, bye!"

"You're weird, Fernando Goldberg," said Janice.

"Yeah, you're weird, Fernando Goldberg," repeated Winnie. And they headed down the hall.

Fern returned to the closet to join Lester. There was just one problem. . . .

Lester wasn't there!

Fern was baffled. "What the . . . !"

He started to feel sick to his stomach.

"This makes absolutely no sense."

He was becoming dizzy from all of the madness.

"Just when you think things can't get any crazier, they . . ."

He leaned against a closet wall to avoid passing out, but . . .

"Whoa!"

The wall gave way, and he found himself collapsing onto a hidden slide.

He descended the slide backward, whipping around corners, heading toward who knows where. It reminded him of the gigantic slide he had slid down at the Gordonville Slide & Splash Water Village, except that this slide was completely dark, had no water in it, and probably didn't have a pool waiting for him at the bottom.

If I don't make it out of this alive, it was nice knowing you, Fern said to himself. Same here, Fern said back to himself just before reaching the end.

# 13

## WHERE THE PROBLEM STEMS FROM

"Oof!" Fern grunted as his face was introduced to the ground.

**SMACK!**

He got up carefully and looked around. Whoa, he thought. What is this place?

The room he'd fallen into wasn't any ordinary room. It was an enormous lab filled with all kinds of test tubes and vials and bubbling potions. But unlike other labs, this lab had something other labs didn't have—food!

All around were meats and cheeses and fruits and vegetables and breads and pastas and nuts and cookies and cakes and every other food you can imagine. But one food stood out from the rest—eggplants! Not the freaky oversize human eggplants of the kind Ms. Durbindin and Principal Hamstone had turned into, but the regular little normal-type eggplants that you see in the grocery store.

They were everywhere.

Fern stood up on a table to get a good look around.

What he found was Lester. His friend was
at the far end of the lab, lying on a long table.

"Typical," Fern called out to Lester.

Lester lifted his head and looked at Fern.
He was wearing a shiny helmet with a ton of
wires sticking out of it.

"What are you wearing that for?" asked Fern as he walked toward Lester. "Come on, get up, and let's get out of here."

"I can't! I need your help!"

"Why?"

Fern heard a voice from behind him answer, "Because his arms and legs are chained to that eggplanting table."

Fern turned around to find himself standing across from Dr. Ned-Grant.

"Yup, that's why," said Lester.

"Dr. Ned-Grant," said Fern, "what are you doing here?"

"I'm building my eggplant army."

"What? Why?" Fern asked.

"So that I can seize control of the school and then conquer the world, so people will finally learn to honor and respect eggplants as they deserve to be honored and respected."

"Don't you think there's a better, less nutso way to do that?" asked Fern. "Like maybe giving a bunch of lectures or something? I mean, building an eggplant army . . . that's insane."

Dr. Ned-Grant started breathing heavily. "Everyone makes fun of eggplants, but the last laugh will be on them, because eggplants are more powerful than anyone can ever imagine.

No one understands that now. But they will."
Dr. Ned-Grant cackled like the mad food
scientist that he had become. "Oh, they will!
HA-HA-HA! And I'm going to get the two of
you to help me."

"How are you going to do that?" Fern
asked.

"By zapping your brain waves into my
eggplants and their brain waves into you!"

"So that's why all our teachers and
classmates are turning into eggplants?" said
Fern. "Because you've been giving your
eggplants their brain waves?"

"Exactly," said Dr. Ned-Grant.

"And all they get in return are squishy,
oval, purple eggplant brain waves, which is
why they're all pretty much useless."

"Making it that much easier for me to
conquer you!" said Dr. Ned-Grant as he

pulled a human-size net out from behind his back.

"And I'll bet you've been using that thing to capture them," said Fern.

"Very smart," said Dr. Ned-Grant. "You've got a big old brain there, buddy boy. You're going to make some eggplant very, very happy."

Dr. Ned-Grant swung the net down at Fern.

"Fern, look out!" yelled Lester.

Fern dodged the net. "And after you catch them, you bring them down here," said Fern.

"You catch on quick," Dr. Ned-Grant said. "But not as quick as I'm going to catch you." He swung the net down again.

"Look out! Look out!" yelled Lester.

Fern dodged the net again.

"And as soon as you're done, you send them back out into the world and let the final effects of your procedure take effect."

"Wow, you're smart," said Dr. Ned-Grant. "You must get really good grades."

"I do okay," said Fern. "I'm not very good at spelling."

"Well, don't worry," said Dr. Ned-Grant. "Spelling won't matter once you're AN EGGPLANT!"

Dr. Ned-Grant threw the net at Fern.

"Be careful, Fern!" yelled Lester.

Fern ducked.

The net went flying into a table of vials and jars.

*Crash!*

Dr. Ned-Grant ran at Fern.

"He's running at you, Fern!" yelled Lester.

"I can see that!" said Fern as he turned and ran from Dr. Ned-Grant. "You don't have to keep telling me every time he does something! I can see!"

Dr. Ned-Grant followed right behind him.

"He's running after you, Fern!" yelled Lester.

Fern zigzagged his way around the lab, trying to lose the doctor. But the doctor still followed close behind.

Fern whizzed down an aisle of carrot peelers.

Dr. Ned-Grant whizzed down the aisle of carrot peelers.

Fern jumped over a giant pile of peppers.

Dr. Ned-Grant jumped over the giant pile of peppers.

Fern slid around a giant mixing bowl.

Dr. Ned-Grant slid around the giant mixing bowl.

"You can't lose me!" the doctor called out to Fern. "You may be young, but I'm in great shape! I always eat right."

*Thud!*

The doctor was so busy telling Fern how physically fit he was that he stopped looking where he was going and ran into an oven and got his head stuck inside.

Fern ran to the other end of the lab and slithered behind a refrigerator.

By the time the doctor got his head out of

the oven, he couldn't find Fern anywhere.

"I know you're in here," Dr. Ned-Grant called out.

Fern didn't answer.

"He isn't here," said Lester. "I saw him leave."

"Who asked you?" said Dr. Ned-Grant to Lester. He called out to Fern. "There's no point in hiding, so you might as well come out now!"

"Don't come out, Fern!" yelled Lester.

"I thought you said he left," said Dr. Ned-Grant.

"Oh," said Lester, "I did. I just . . . I just . . . I just wanted to trick you. He did leave. And that's why he's not going to come out now."

Fern stayed right where he was.

"Okay, fine," said Dr. Ned-Grant. "I'll deal with him later. In the meantime"—he looked at Lester—"I have other business to attend to."

"And what might that be?" asked Lester.

Dr. Ned-Grant smiled. "You."

Lester gulped. "I was afraid that's what you were going to say."

# 14
## TRANSFOODMATION

Dr. Ned-Grant grabbed some cables and brought them over to an eggplant on a table next to the table Lester was lying on.

Dr. Ned-Grant attached the cables to the eggplant.

*Click.*

He turned to Lester and laughed.

"You don't scare me," said Lester.

Dr. Ned-Grant walked toward Lester with the cables.

Lester started to cry. "I take it back. You do scare me! You do scare me!"

Fern peeked around the refrigerator and watched the entire horrifying scene unfold.

Dr. Ned-Grant reached down over Lester, holding the cables.

"This won't hurt a bit," he said. "It will hurt a *lot*! Ah! HA-HA-HA!"

That would've been the perfect moment for Fern to jump out as Super Chicken Nugget Boy and save the day. There was just one problem—he didn't have any ketchup! Lester was always the one with ketchup, and he was a little busy at that moment.

"No! Please, *NO!*" screamed Lester. "How about if I just pretend to be an eggplant? That could be just as good. Maybe even better, because you'd save on the electricity."

"Not a chance," said Dr. Ned-Grant.

He clipped the cables on to the wires sticking out of Lester's helmet.

*Click!*

"AAHHH!" Lester cried out.

There's got to be something I can do, Fern thought.

He slammed his elbow into the back of the refrigerator in frustration.

*Thud!*

He felt something smash into his leg.

*Squish!*

He looked down. It was a tomato.

Great. Just great, he thought. My best friend's about to be turned into an eggplant and I'm sitting here getting hit by tomatoes.

Dr. Ned-Grant walked over to his electric eggplant transformation station, singing in delight.

♫ TURNING PEOPLE INTO EGGPLANTS ♪
IS WHAT I LOVE TO DO.
I LOVE TO SEE THEM TURN ALL PURPLE
WITH STEMS THAT THEY JUST GREW.

"You're mad!" yelled Lester.

"I know," Dr. Ned-Grant yelled back. "I'm a *mad* food scientist. DUH! Now let's get this show on the road."

"NO-O-O-O!!!" Lester cried.

Fern looked down. He couldn't stand to watch. That's when he noticed something very interesting: breading was forming on his

leg where the tomato had fallen onto him.

Of course, Fern thought. The squished tomato is reacting with my inner Super Chicken Nugget powers!

Fern banged his elbow into the back of the refrigerator again.

*Thud!*

Sure enough . . .

*Squish!*

A tomato landed on his arm.

A second later, just as he had hoped, a light, flaky breading appeared there.

Out in the laboratory, Dr. Ned-Grant flicked all sorts of switches and turned tons of knobs.

Lasers and electric sounds echoed throughout the lab.

*Bizz! Wawa! Wayyyy! Bleep! Bleep!*

"Do you hear that?" Dr. Ned-Grant called out. "It's the sweet sounds of my eggplant empire coming to life!"

Fern wasn't paying attention to the doctor, though. He was too busy.

He banged against the fridge again.

*Thud!*

*Squish! Squish! Squish!*

Three more tomatoes landed on him: one on his left leg, one on his chest, and one on his back.

He kept going as, out in the lab, Lester

screamed for mercy. "PLEASE!!!! DON'T!!!!"

"And now for my favorite part of the procedure," said Dr. Ned-Grant, "the flip of the Final Phase Transformation Toggle. HA-HA-HA!"

"You'll never get away with this," said Lester.

"It sure looks like I will," said Dr. Ned-Grant as he moved to unlock the giant stainless-steel safe that housed the Final Phase Transformation Toggle.

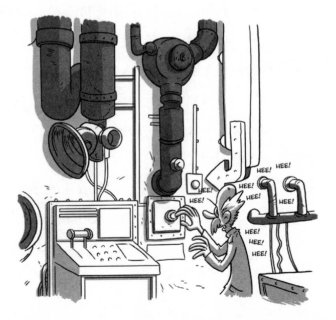

"NO-O-O-O-O!!!"

"Don't worry, Lester, I'm coming," Fern whispered to himself.

He jumped out from behind the refrigerator, completely covered in breading and ready to do battle with Dr. Ned-Grant. But Dr. Ned-Grant didn't notice him. He was too busy trying to unlock the safe. Which was a good thing for Fern, because just then he realized that he wasn't supersize!

He wondered what could've gone wrong.

On the other side of the lab, Dr. Ned-Grant struggled to open the Final Phase Transformation Toggle lock.

"Rats! Thing is stuck!" said Dr. Ned-Grant.

"Ha!" said Lester. "I told you you'd never get away with this."

"Don't worry," said Dr. Ned-Grant. "It's nothing a little vinegar won't loosen up."

That's it! Fern realized. That's what's missing—vinegar and all the other ingredients in ketchup!

Dr. Ned-Grant grabbed a bottle of vinegar from a nearby shelf while Fern crept over to a spice rack and quickly grabbed the salt, sugar, onion powder, and allspice.

"HA-HA! This'll do the trick," said Dr. Ned-Grant. "You'll be an eggplant in no time, and then your cowardly friend will be next! HA-HA-HA!"

"Never!" yelled Lester.

Dr. Ned-Grant poured vinegar all over the Final Phase Transformation Toggle lock.

Fern poured salt, sugar, onion powder, and allspice all over himself.

Dr. Ned-Grant set the vinegar down and turned the Final Phase Transformation Toggle lock.

*Click.*

It opened.

Dr. Ned-Grant turned to Lester. "Get ready, my friend, for a permanent eggplant experience! HA-HA-HA-HA!"

Dr. Ned-Grant reached for the toggle.

Fern ran up behind Dr. Ned-Grant, grabbed the vinegar, and poured it all over himself.

"This is my favorite part," said Dr. Ned-

Grant. He grabbed hold of the toggle switch and started to pull down. But before he could finish the job . . .

*Kerblam!*

# 15
## PUNY PURPLE PEOPLE

"Super Chicken Nugget Boy!" said Dr. Ned-Grant. "Where did you come from?"

"Where I came from isn't as important as

where you're going," said Super Chicken Nugget Boy.

"Oh, really?" said Dr. Ned-Grant. "And where might that be?"

"Straight to the slammer!" yelled Lester.

"HA-HA!" laughed Dr. Ned-Grant.

"I'm afraid he's right, Dr. Ned-Grant," said Super Chicken Nugget Boy. "Your days of eggplant insanity are over."

"That's a good one," said Dr. Ned-Grant. "It's so funny that I almost forgot to laugh, except that I didn't. HA-HA-HA! . . . Now, if you'll excuse me, I've got to turn this boy into an eggplant."

Dr. Ned-Grant turned back to the Final Phase Transformation Toggle and grabbed it.

Super Chicken Nugget Boy's hand landed on top of Dr. Ned-Grant's. "If I were you,

I'd let go of that Final Phase Transformation Toggle," he said.

"And if I were you I'd let go of my hand," said Dr. Ned-Grant.

"Well, I'm not, so what are you going to do about it?" Super Chicken Nugget Boy said.

"Since you asked, I guess I'll have to show you," the doctor replied. "I was hoping it wouldn't come to this, but . . . Who am I kidding? I've been dying for it to come to this."

Dr. Ned-Grant tilted his head up to the ceiling and called out, "Eggplants, awaken!"

All at once, the seemingly normal little eggplants in the lab opened their eyes.

"AAAHH!" screamed Lester.

"Whoa!" said Super Chicken Nugget Boy.

"I didn't know eggplants had eyes," said Lester.

"Because they don't," said Dr. Ned-Grant,

". . . usually. These are my special eggplants. The ones I created with the brain waves of students and teachers at Bert Lahr Elementary School. The ones I created to seize the school and conquer the WORLD! HA-HA-HA!"

"It's going to take a lot more than just eggplants with eyes to stop Super Chicken Nugget Boy from saving the day," said Lester.

"Oh, I know," said Dr. Ned-Grant. "That's why they have more than just eyes." He called out, "Eggplants, seize Super Chicken Nugget Boy!"

All the eggplants suddenly stood up on little eggplant legs. Little eggplant arms popped out of their sides, and at the end of every arm were little eggplant hands and fingers.

Within moments, eggplants were charging at Super Chicken Nugget Boy from every direction. One dived off a shelf and landed on Super Chicken Nugget Boy's head.

"Yikes!" shouted Super Chicken Nugget Boy. "Purple pest, crawling near brain."

He grabbed the eggplant and threw it across the room.

*Crash!*

Another eggplant bounced off the ground and slammed into Super Chicken Nugget Boy's gut.

"I don't know if I've got the stomach for this," said Super Chicken Nugget Boy. He pushed his stomach muscles out and sent the eggplant sailing into an oncoming pack of eggplants. "Oh, I guess I do," he laughed.

Four more eggplants snuck up behind him and started poking their rough green stems into his breading.

*Biff! Bash! Stab! Stick!*

Super Chicken Nugget Boy danced around as if he had ants in his pants. "Not fun! Not fun! Not fun! Not fun!"

"Don't worry! You got 'em, Nug!" cheered Lester.

"The only thing he's got is PROBLEMS," said Dr. Ned-Grant. "HA-HA-HA!"

More eggplants started climbing up Super Chicken Nugget Boy.

He stomped around the room, trying to shake them off. "SHAKE! SHAKE! SHAKE

THE EGGPLANTS OFF! SHAKE! SHAKE! SHAKE THE EGGPLANTS OFF!"

Another eggplant planted itself over Super Chicken Nugget Boy's eyes like a blindfold.

Super Chicken Nugget Boy smashed into a wall.

*Smoosh!*

One of the eggplants got squished between the wall and Super Chicken Nugget Boy's body. "Is that the sweet sound of squishing I hear?" asked Super Chicken Nugget Boy.

"It sure is," said Lester.

Super Chicken Nugget Boy started rolling his body all over the wall and squishing the eggplants that were hanging on to him.

*Squish! Squish! Smoosh! Squish!*

He squished all the eggplants, except the one covering his face. He tried to grab it, but he couldn't get a good grip, so instead . . .

*Bash!*

He rammed his head into the wall.

*Smoosh!*

The squished eggplant slid slowly down to the floor.

"That's using your head!" said Dr. Ned-Grant. "HA-HA-HA!"

Super Chicken Nugget Boy turned around to face the room, dizzy from bashing his head into the wall. "Ooh, boy, anybody got an aspirin?" he said as he watched dozens of eggplants rush toward him.

He tried kicking and hitting the oncoming eggplants, but it was no use: the dizziness had thoroughly thrown off his balance. He kept missing the eggplants while more and more of them just kept coming. Before he knew it, Super Chicken Nugget Boy had dozens and dozens of eggplants crawling all over him.

"I thought eggplants were supposed to be good for you," he called out.

"They may not be good for you," said Dr. Ned-Grant, "but they sure are good for me. HA-HA-HA!"

The eggplants kept coming.

There were eggplants hanging on to eggplants hanging on to eggplants hanging on to Super Chicken Nugget Boy, and there was absolutely nothing he could do about it. He was too dizzy, too drained, and too outnumbered.

He wobbled to the left.

He wobbled to the right.

He spun around.

He fell over.

Lester screamed, "NO-O-O-O-O-O-O-O!"

# 16
## THE EGGSCAPE

Super Chicken Nugget Boy lay chained to a table next to Lester's table, weak from the battle.

Dr. Ned-Grant stood on top of a gigantic freezer, surrounded by eggplants that were standing like soldiers preparing for battle.

"Excellent work, my purple pets!" said Dr. Ned-Grant. "We've defeated our greatest enemy, Super Chicken Nugget Boy!"

The eggplants raised their eggplant hands in victory.

"Now there's nothing standing between us and conquering the world!"

The eggplants jumped up and down for joy.

"Let's not waste another second. The time has come for you to take your rightful place as emperors of the earth! Onward, eggplants! Onward!"

The eggplants began marching out through the giant lab door.

"This isn't good," Lester whispered.

"You got that right," Super Chicken Nugget Boy whispered back. "And yet, maybe not quite as bad as you think."

"What do you mean?" Lester whispered.

"I can feel the ketchup starting to wear off," whispered Super Chicken Nugget Boy.

"That's terrible," whispered Lester.

"Maybe not," whispered Super Chicken Nugget Boy.

"Huh?" said Lester as he watched Super Chicken Nugget Boy's breading fall off and his body morph back into Fern's body.

"We're doomed," said Lester.

Fern slipped his hands out of the handcuffs that had been clamped tightly on to Super Chicken Nugget Boy's thick, breaded wrists but were way too big for Fern's own skinny ones.

"You're out! You're loose! You're unattached!" said Lester.

Fern nodded.

He grabbed a nearby key and unlocked Lester while Dr. Ned-Grant was busy cheering his marching mass of eggplants on. "That's it, eggplants! Off you go! Be bold! Be strong! Be seedy!"

"Let's get out of here," said Fern.

"Where are we going?" asked Lester.

"To save the world from the eggplant invasion," said Fern.

"How are we going to do that? As far as I can tell, there's only one way out of here, and at the moment it's being used by an extremely large eggplant army."

"You've got a point," said Fern. Then he

noticed the eggplants that had been squished against the wall.

He reached out, grabbed a bunch, and handed them to Lester. "Here! Rub these all over your body."

"Are you nuts? Why on earth would I—"

*Splat!*

Fern flung the eggplants at Lester, covering him in purple from head to toe.

"Hey!" said Lester.

Fern smeared the insides of a bunch of eggplants all over himself.

"Now, act like an eggplant and follow me," said Fern.

"Oh, I get it," said Lester.

Fern and Lester walked up to a group of eggplants on their way out of the lab and started waddling alongside them.

They marched toward the exit, where Dr. Ned-Grant stood shouting encouragement.

"Excellent, eggplants! Excellent!"

They were just about to head through the door of the lab when Dr. Ned-Grant spotted them. "Whoa!" he shouted. "Hold it right there."

They stopped in their tracks.

Dr. Ned-Grant looked them up and down.

They held their breath.

"You certainly are a couple of enormous eggplants," said Dr. Ned-Grant.

Their hearts sank.

Dr. Ned-Grant laughed. "HA-HA-HA! The bigger the better, that's what I always say! Off you go, eggplants!"

Fern and Lester breathed sighs of relief and headed through the giant lab door.

They marched with the eggplants down a long, dark hallway, up some stairs, down some stairs, then up some more stairs, and finally up through a manhole, which left them smack-dab in the middle of the school playground.

# 17
## COMPLETE PLANTAMONIUM

It was massive mayhem on the playground! Eggplants were everywhere! Students screamed in horror! Teachers trembled with fear! And the eggplant people, like Ms. Durbindin and Donna Wergnort and Principal Hamstone, ran around in circles, unsure of whose side they were on.

The evil eggplant soldiers attacked anyone and everyone who crossed their path.

"HELP! SAVE US!" screamed a group of third grade girls as

they ran from an eggplant stampede.

In one corner of the playground, a first grade boy whimpered and wailed as an eggplant hung off the top of his head. "This eggplant has got its stinking stem stuck in my scalp! Aaaaaghhhhh!"

Another pack of eggplants played *Bowling for Teachers*, rolling into teachers and seeing how many they could knock over.

"What do we do now?" asked Lester.

"Follow me," said Fern as he headed toward the school.

"Follow me! Follow me! All you ever say is 'Follow me,'" said Lester.

"Okay, you can stay here with the eggplants if you'd like," said Fern.

Just then, Farnsworth Yorb raced by, screaming, with a pack of angry eggplants hot on his trail. "Mommy! Daddy! Sister!

Granny! Hhhhhhellllllpppppp!"

"On second thought," said Lester, "I think I'll follow you."

Fern and Lester ran into Ms. Durbindin's classroom.

"Quick!" said Fern as he ran toward the back of the room. "Throw me some ketchup packets from your desk!"

"What's the point?" asked Lester as he pulled the ketchup out. "There's just too many of them, even for Super Chicken Nugget Boy. Remember? You didn't exactly save the day back in that lab."

"Maybe not . . ." said Fern.

Lester threw the ketchup packets to him.

Fern caught them.

He pulled Arnie out of his tank.

"But with Arnie the Awesome Amphibian, it's a whole different ball game!"

He squirted himself and Arnie with ketchup.

*Kerblam!*

Super Chicken Nugget Boy and Arnie the Awesome Amphibian were back in business.

"Come on," said Super Chicken Nugget Boy. "It's time these awful eggplants were eliminated once and for all!"

# 18
## ARNIE UPCHUCK

Super Chicken Nugget Boy and Lester rode out onto the playground on Arnie the Awesome Amphibian's back.

"I hope you're hungry," said Super Chicken Nugget Boy.

"Are you kidding? I'm starving," said Lester.

"I'm not talking to you."

"Then who are you talking to?"

"Him," said Super Chicken Nugget Boy, pointing down at Arnie the Awesome Amphibian.

Just then, Arnie the Awesome Amphibian

dipped his head and sucked a dozen eggplants up into his mouth!

*Slurp!*

"Whoa!" Lester called out.

Arnie bit down.

*Chomp! Chomp!*

"HE'S EATING THEM!" said Lester.

"I know," said Super Chicken Nugget Boy.

Arnie swallowed the eggplants.

*Gulp!*

"How did you know he liked eating eggplants?" asked Lester.

"Because he started eating Ms. Durbindin that day she turned into one."

"Oh, yeah," said Lester. "Of course."

"Now, let's finish off these petrifying plants of egg before it's too late!" said Super Chicken Nugget Boy. "To the left, Arnie! To the left!"

Arnie turned left and ran into another group of eggplants.

*Slurp!*

*Chomp! Chomp! Chomp!*

*Gulp!*

And just like that, the eggplants were gone.

"WOO-HOO!" screamed Lester.

"Attaboy, Arnie! Attaboy!" said Super Chicken Nugget Boy. "Now, straight ahead!"

Arnie ran toward a group of eggplants that had Roy Clapmist surrounded.

He sucked them up.

*Slurp!*

*Chomp!*

"YOW!"

≥YOW!≤

GRUMBLE GURGLE

"Whoa," said Lester. "What was that 'yow'?"

"What 'yow'? From where?" Super Chicken Nugget Boy asked.

"I think it was coming from inside Arnie."

*Chomp!*

"There it is again," said Lester.

"Uh-oh!" said Super Chicken Nugget Boy.

*Gulp!*

Super Chicken Nugget Boy and Lester looked at each other and called out in horror, "ROY!"

"Arnie must've slurped him up with the eggplants," said Super Chicken Nugget Boy.

"NO-O-O-O-O!" Lester cried.

"Poor Roy," said Super Chicken Nugget Boy. "He was a good guy. He didn't deserve to die in the mouth of a supersize salamander."

*Gurgle! Cough! Burp! Blech!*

Arnie suddenly spat Roy out, sending him flying over the playground!

*Whizz!*

*Aaaghhh!*

Roy landed on top of a bunch of eggplants, squishing them to death.

He stood up and waved to Super Chicken Nugget Boy and Lester. "I'm okay! I'm okay. Just a little"—he spun around and fell on the ground again—"woozy."

"All right," said Super Chicken Nugget Boy, "let's turn it around, Arnie!"

Arnie turned around and ran toward another gang of eggplants.

"Eat up, buddy boy!" said Super Chicken Nugget Boy.

*Slurp!*

Arnie sucked them all up.

"Mmmm! Yummy!" said Lester.

Arnie dropped his head and moaned. "URRGGH."

"Oh, no!" said Lester.

"Don't worry," said Super Chicken Nugget Boy.

Arnie opened his mouth, and all the eggplants rolled out.

"Now can I worry?" asked Lester.

"Yes," said Super Chicken Nugget Boy."

"What's wrong with him?!"

"I'm not sure. Maybe eating Roy made him nauseous."

Arnie moaned again.

"Yeah, that must be it," said Super Chicken Nugget Boy.

"Terrific! Arnie the Awesome Amphibian has

awesome indigestion! What do we do now?"

"SURRENDER!" a voice called out from behind them.

Super Chicken Nugget Boy and Lester spun around.

Dr. Ned-Grant was standing on top of the jungle gym.

"Never!" yelled Lester.

"Don't be foolish!" said Dr. Ned-Grant. "You know you're no match for my invincible eggplants!"

"Oh, yeah?" said Super Chicken Nugget Boy. "I've got a plan that's going to obliterate you and your entire eggplant army."

"HA-HA-HA! That's a good one!" laughed Dr. Ned-Grant.

"What's your plan?" Lester whispered to Super Chicken Nugget Boy.

"I don't have one," Super Chicken Nugget

Boy whispered back. "I just thought that would sound good."

"Seize them!" Dr. Ned-Grant called out to his eggplants.

All at once, eggplants from all over the playground started running toward Lester, Arnie, and Super Chicken Nugget Boy.

"Quick, Arnie!" yelled Super Chicken Nugget Boy. "Retreat!"

Arnie tried galloping away from the eggplants, but his upset stomach slowed him down.

"Great! Just great!" Lester cried out. "Here I am, about to get mowed down by a mob of bloodthirsty eggplants, and all I've got to protect me is a simpleminded superhero and an oversize salamander that can't keep its food down!"

"Hey! That's not a bad idea!" said Super Chicken Nugget Boy.

"What's not a bad idea?" asked Lester.

The eggplants were getting closer.

"Climb into Arnie!" cried Super Chicken Nugget Boy.

"Excuse me?"

"Climb into Arnie!"

"But . . ."

The eggplants kept coming.

Super Chicken Nugget Boy grabbed Lester by the collar and lifted him up.

"Open wide, Arnie!"

Lester protested. "Hey! Wait just a . . ."

Super Chicken Nugget Boy flung Lester into Arnie's mouth.

"All right, Arnie, do your thing!" said Super Chicken Nugget Boy.

*Gurgle! Cough! Burp! Blech!*

Lester flew out of Arnie's mouth!

*Whizz!*

"AAAGHHH!"

He flew headfirst into the pack of approaching eggplants.

"Bull's-eye!" exclaimed Super Chicken Nugget Boy.

"Blast!" screamed Dr. Ned-Grant.

"What now?" Super Chicken Nugget Boy asked Arnie as another barbaric bunch of eggplants raced toward them. "Oh, yeah, that's right. You're a salamander. You can't talk. Shoot!"

"HA-HA-HA!" laughed Dr. Ned-Grant. "Let's see how you get out of this one."

Just then, Ms. Durbindin (the eggplant version) wobbled over near Super Chicken Nugget Boy and Arnie. Super Chicken Nugget Boy grabbed her.

"I feel just sick about this, Ms. Durbindin," said Super Chicken Nugget Boy, "but I can't let these evil eggplants inherit the earth."

He threw Ms. Durbindin into Arnie the Awesome Amphibian's mouth. "I hope this doesn't affect my grade."

*Gurgle! Cough! Burp! Blech!*

Ms. Durbindin flew out of Arnie's mouth.

*Whizz!*

"AAAGHHH!"

*Thump!*

*Splat!*

She smashed right into the barbaric bunch of eggplants, and a monstrous amount of eggplant juice splashed into the air.

"Whoa!" said Roy Clapmist.

"Gadzooks!" said Lester.

"This chicken's really choking my chain," grumbled Dr. Ned-Grant.

When the eggplant juice settled, something spectacular was left standing there—it was MS. DURBINDIN! And not the weird half-woman, half-eggplant Ms. Durbindin, either, but the good old-fashioned human Ms. Durbindin.

Super Chicken Nugget Boy gasped.

"Look, Arnie! The power of the impact punctured her eggplant pod and returned her to normal."

"THIS IS BAAAAAAAAAD!" shrieked Dr. Ned-Grant.

"How strange," said Ms. Durbindin, looking around at the squished-up eggplants. Then she noticed all the other eggplants chasing everyone around the playground. "My

goodness," she said, "what in good golly is going on here?"

"We'll explain later," said Lester, running toward her. "But right now we'd better get out of the way. I've got a funny feeling it's about to start raining eggplant people!"

Lester was right.

Super Chicken Nugget Boy started scooping up all the eggplant people on the playground: Donna Wergnort, Mr. Pummel, and Kenny Brack, and all the rest, until every last eggplant was smashed and shattered to smithereens, and every eggplant person was back to normal. All except for one, that is.

With his precious eggplant army destroyed, Dr. Ned-Grant did what any brilliant, mad food scientist would do under the circumstances—HE RAN!

# 19
## THE MAD DASH

Dr. Ned-Grant ran from the playground carrying the one-and-only eggplant person who was left—Principal Hamstone.

"Quick, Super Chicken Nugget Boy!" yelled Lester, who had made it safely to the top of the school. "He's getting away!"

"UH-UH!" said Super Chicken Nugget Boy. "Not on my watch!"

He looked for someone to fire at Dr. Ned-Grant, but there was no one around. Everyone had run for cover during the eggplant-person shower.

Meanwhile, Dr. Ned-Grant was getting farther and farther away from the school.

"HA-HA-HA! They think they've seen the last of us," he said to the eggplant version of Principal Hamstone, "but they're sorely mistaken. In the end, THE EGGPLANTS WILL PREVAIL! THE EGGPLANTS WILL PREVAIL!"

Suddenly, Super Chicken Nugget Boy heard strange whimpering sounds coming from the bushes behind him. He pushed aside some branches and discovered Dirk and Snort sobbing like little babies. "Wah-wah-wah, boo-hoo-hoo, mama-mama-mama-mama . . ."

"You guys are even bigger chickens than I am," said Super Chicken Nugget Boy.

"Are not," said Dirk.

"Oh, yeah? Prove it," said Super Chicken Nugget Boy. "Arnie—"

Arnie opened his mouth.

"Get in," said Super Chicken Nugget Boy.

"Are you nuts?" asked Dirk.

"Maybe," said Super Chicken Nugget Boy as he grabbed Dirk and Snort, "but not as nuts as that mad menace who wants to turn the entire world into a giant eggplant party."

Super Chicken Nugget Boy threw Dirk and Snort into Arnie's mouth.

"You'll be hearing from my dad about this," said Dirk.

"Yeah, if he's not an eggplant for the rest of his life," said Super Chicken Nugget Boy. "Fire away, Arnie!"

*Gurgle! Cough! Burp!*

Arnie opened his mouth and fired.

*BLECH!*

Dirk and Snort were sent hurtling through the air.

*Whizz!*

Dr. Ned-Grant ran as fast as he could from the two flying fourth graders.

"AAAGHHH!" they screamed.

"NO-O-O-O-O-O-O-O-O-!!!" he screamed.

But he wasn't fast enough.

Dirk smashed into the mad scientist, knocking Principal Hamstone the eggplant out of his hands.

Snort followed with the knockout punch, landing right on top of Dr. Ned-Grant.

Principal Hamstone's eggplant exterior was ripped away, leaving the original Principal Hamstone sitting there, stunned.

"As I said," said Principal Hamstone,

"there's absolutely nothing to worry about. None of us are going to be turned into eggplants."

Dr. Ned-Grant moaned in agony.

# 20
## DIRK SCAMSTONE

A crowd of teachers and kids surrounded Dirk and Snort as the cops took Dr. Ned-Grant off to the slammer.

"Don't blame me!" screamed Dr. Ned-Grant as he was being dragged away. "It's the talking eggplant's fault! He made me do it!"

"Sure, buddy

boy, whatever you say," said one of the cops.

"Yeah," said the other cop, "I know how you feel. I once had a peach tell me to steal a million dollars."

"Really?" asked Dr. Ned-Grant.

"No, you nut job," said the cop. "Now, get in the squad car."

Fern walked up to the crowd.

"Where were you?" asked Roy Clapmist.

"He was probably sniveling in the bushes like a little baby," said Dirk.

"Yeah!" said Snort. *Snort! Snort!*

The other kids laughed.

"You missed all the action," said Lester.

"Yeah," said Dirk. "I caught Dr. Ned-Grant and saved the world."

"And me, too," said Snort.

"Wow," said Fern.

"They couldn't have done it without Super

Chicken Nugget Boy," said Winnie Kinney.

"Yeah, he's the real hero," said Lester.

"Whatever," said Dirk. "It's the same difference, since we're, like, best friends now, me and Super Chicken Nugget Boy." He turned to Fern. "Oh, and he wanted me to tell you that he doesn't want to be friends with you anymore because you were too chicken to come out and battle the eggplant army. Hey, that's funny. You're too chicken to be friends with a chicken. Heh-heh-heh!"

Snort snorted. *Snort! Snort!*

"Anyway," said Dirk, "he said you really embarrassed him. Unlike me, who made him proud."

"He's not the only one you made proud," chimed in Principal Hamstone. "I'm very, very proud of you, son."

"Thank you, Papa," said Dirk.

"So proud," Principal Hamstone continued, "that I'm canceling the remainder of your detention."

"Are you sure, Papa?" asked Dirk, with a big, fake, innocent look on his face.

"Absolutely," said Principal Hamstone. "And I'm going to cancel Snort's detention while I'm at it. I mean, Donald's. Sorry."

"That's okay. Call me Donald. Call me Snort. Call me whatever you want, so long as you don't call me to detention!" said Snort. "WOO-HOO!"

Fern and Lester walked away from the crowd.

"Why did you let him get away with saying that he was best friends with Super Chicken Nugget Boy?" asked Lester.

"Why not?" Fern said.

"Because it's not true."

"Yeah, and everybody knows that."

"But still . . ."

"It's like when Rudy Fillmersk said he ate

four medium pizzas and drank twelve orange sodas," said Fern. "We all knew he was lying."

"No, he wasn't," said Lester. "I watched him do it."

"Really?"

"Yeah. I also watched him throw up for six hours afterward."

"Huh . . ." said Fern.

# 21

## ANOTHER DAY, ANOTHER CHICKEN

After school, on the day following the big eggplant invasion, Fern, Lester, and Roy Clapmist were on the playground playing How-Would-You-Walk-if-You-Were-an-Alien?

Roy was in the middle of an impressive crouching-alien waddle that he called the "Duck, Duck, Martian," when Lester called out. "UH-OH!"

Roy sprang back up to a standing position.

"What is it?" asked Fern.

"Look," said Lester, pointing at Dirk and Snort exiting the school.

Roy's smile quickly turned into a frown. "Oh, that's right," he said. "No more detention for them."

Dirk and Snort headed right toward them.

"Well, it was nice while it lasted," said Lester. "What should we do?"

"I don't know," said Fern. "Pray?"

Lester gritted his teeth.

Roy closed his eyes and started praying.

Fern took a deep breath and braced himself for what he was sure was coming next—another miserable run-in with Dirk Hamstone.

But then something completely unexpected happened: Dirk stuck out his hand to Fern, smiled, and said, "Can we just stop fighting and finally be friends?"

Just kidding!

That would be way too bizarre. What did happen, though, was almost as bizarre.

A gigantic mug with feet went speeding past the school. It was filled with puppies, and a woman was running after it.

"HELP! HELP!" yelled the woman. "That mugger just stole my poochies."

"Whoa," Fern said to Dirk and Snort. "You guys had better get going."

"What is that supposed to mean?" Dirk asked.

"Aren't you going to get your friend Super Chicken Nugget Boy and save the day?"

"Oh," said Dirk. "Uh, yeah . . . I guess . . . I guess we'd better go do that. Come on, Snorton!"

Dirk started running.

"Where are you going? The mug went that way," Snort said, pointing in the other direction.

"Just come on!" yelled Dirk, and Snort ran off with him.

Lester and Roy cracked up.

"That was a great one!" said Lester.

"Yeah," said Roy. "Now, let's follow that woman and see what happens when Super Chicken Nugget Boy shows up."

"He's not going to," said Lester.

"How do you know?" Roy asked.

"Because the police can take care of this one," he said.

"You don't know that," said Roy.

"Yes I do," said Lester.

"How?" Roy asked.

"Because I know Super Chicken Nugget

Boy better than anyone," said Lester.

"You always say that," said Roy. "But nobody really knows Super Chicken Nugget Boy. He's a mystery."

"Oh, yeah? Well, guess what?" said Lester.

"What?"

"Super Chicken Nugget Boy is . . ."

"Hey, wait a second," said Roy, looking around. "Where did Fern go?"

"I don't know," said Lester. "He must've . . ."

Just then, Super Chicken Nugget Boy burst onto the playground, riding on Arnie.

"Don't worry, ma'am!" he cried. "That mug won't be making mischief anymore. Not now that Super Chicken Nugget Boy is committed to catching the creepy cup! Yee-haw!"

Roy looked at Lester. "See? I told you so."

"Yeah," said Lester. "I guess you were right. Sometimes he even surprises *me.*"

"Yup," said Roy. "Now, what were you going to tell me about him?"

"Oh . . . nothing," said Lester. "Let's follow him."

The boys started running up the street.

They could hear Super Chicken Nugget Boy off in the distance, calling out: "Have no fear, miss! Your doggie disaster will soon be over! Super Chicken Nugget Boy will make that mugger miserable for his misbehavior."

Super Chicken Nugget Boy was back where he belonged—righting wrongs and crippling crooks with his favorite crime-fighting companion, Arnie the Awesome Amphibian.

The End!